Helping Kids Heal

When Pete's Dad Got Sick

Written by Kathleen Long Bostrom

Illustrated by Cheri Bladholm

Zonderkidz
The children's group of Zondervan

www.zonderkidz.com

When Pete's Dad Got Sick
Copyright © 2004 by The Zondervan Corporation
Illustrations copyright © 2004 by Cheri Bladholm

ISBN: 0-310-70655-6

Requests for information should be addressed to:
Zonderkidz, Grand Rapids, Michigan 49530

All Scripture quotations, unless otherwise indicated, are taken from the HOLY BIBLE, NEW INTERNATIONAL READER'S VERSION ®. Copyright © 1995, 1996, 1998 by International Bible Society. Used by permission of Zondervan. All Rights Reserved.

All rights reserved. No part of this publication may be reproduced, stored in a retrieval system, or transmitted in any form or by any means—electronic, mechanical, photocopy, recording, or any other—except for brief quotations in printed reviews, without the prior permission of the publisher.

Zonderkidz is a trademark of Zondervan.

Editor: Gwen Ellis
Art Direction & Design: Laura M. Maitner

Printed in China
04 05 06 07/HK/4 3 2 1

To Laura, Ken, Jennifer, and Jack

Who show me the truth that we can
indeed do all things through God who strengthens us.

Always, with love,
Kathy

To Jesús Catriel Eduardo, Lucy Mary Luz,
and their parents Lidia Marta and
Luis Alejandro Coronel. Your kindness
and strength brought me such joy.

Cheri Bladholm

PETE COULD REMEMBER when his dad had been like other dads.

"Race you to the house!" Pete's dad would say every time they finished playing outside. Pete's dad was fast, but Pete was always faster. "And the winner is Pete Phillips!" his dad laughed as Pete reached the house first.

Pete's dad would lift him high up into the air, give him a big hug, and say, "You're my best buddy!"

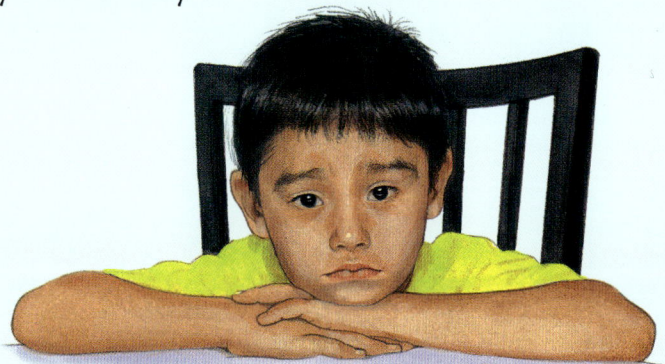

Then Pete's dad began to get sick. At first, his father just walked slower than usual. Then came the days when his father could hardly walk. Some days, he even had to use a wheelchair. Pete didn't like those days at all. He didn't like any of it.

Pete's dad was tired a lot. He sat in his chair and fell asleep long before Pete's bedtime. And he didn't race with Pete anymore.

Pete prayed every night. "Dear God, I'm scared. Please make my daddy well. Help him to run fast again."

But instead of getting better, his dad just got slower. He stayed home more. He tried to take care of Pete and help around the house so Pete's mother could work. But even that got to be too much. People from the church brought meals and cleaned the house and drove Pete back and forth to school.

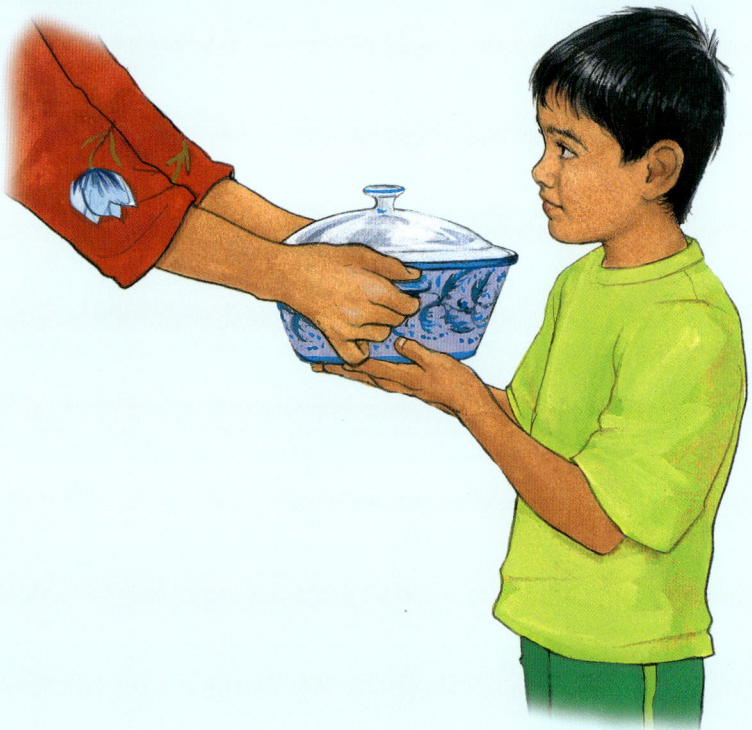

As the days and months went by, it became harder and harder for Pete to remember the fun he'd had with his dad before he got sick.

One day after school, Pete's friend Charlie came to the house to play. It was the first time they had played at Pete's house.

Both boys loved to run. "On your mark, get set, go!" Charlie shouted, and the two boys raced across the yard and back.

"Let's try again," said Charlie, out of breath. "I'll beat you this time."

Then Charlie looked over at the house. There stood Pete's dad, leaning on a cane and watching.

"Pete! Who's that old man in your house?" Charlie asked, nudging Pete and pointing toward the sliding-glass door.

"Oh, that's my dad," said Pete. He wished his father hadn't come to the door to watch them race.

"What's wrong with him?" said Charlie. "Why does he have a cane? And why isn't he at work?"

Pete bristled. "There's nothing wrong with him! Just shut up and go home!" Charlie looked at Pete, then at Pete's dad. He got up without a word, grabbed his jacket, and ran off down the street.

PETE STAYED AWAY from Charlie at school the next day. Or maybe it was the other way around. When Pete got home, he found his dad sitting at the kitchen table.

"What's up, sport?" Pete's dad said as Pete dropped his backpack and coat to the floor.

"Nothing," Pete said.

His dad handed Pete a plate. "I made you a peanut butter and pickle sandwich," he said. "Your favorite."

Pete took a bite but didn't feel much like eating. What he really wanted was to race his dad to the house, then have his dad lift him high up into the air, give him a big hug, and say, "You're my best buddy!"

"I watched you and Charlie race yesterday," his dad said. "You're getting faster all the time."

"What does it matter?" Pete blurted out. "I don't want to race with Charlie, I want to race with you! I want you back the way you were! I want you to be like other dads!" He couldn't stop the words or the tears. He buried his face in his hands, ashamed.

"Pete, Pete, Pete," his dad repeated softly. "It's okay. I want all those things, too. I want to be able to do the things other dads do. The things that you and I used to do."

Pete noticed the tears on his dad's cheek. "Dad?" he whispered. "Will you ever run again?"

His dad sighed. "I don't think so, Pete. There was a time when being a fast runner was the most important thing in the world to me. Not anymore."

"But why would God give you fast legs and then take them away from you?"

"God didn't take them away from me, Pete," his dad said. "Sometimes, people get sick or hurt. I don't know why. I only know that God loves us and wants what is best for us, and that God gives us everything we need. The Bible promises that *'I can do everything by the power of Christ. He gives me strength.'"*

"I guess so," Pete said. "But I still wish you had your fast legs."

Pete's dad placed his hand on Pete's soft hair. "I don't have legs that run, but God's love makes me feel strong. And God has given me something more important than fast legs. I have my best buddy sitting right here on my lap."

PETE'S DAD bent over and picked up a shoebox.

"I don't know why I never showed you these before," his dad said. "I guess because I couldn't bear to look at them myself."

Pete's dad opened the box, took out a medal, and handed it to his son.

"First Place, Track Team," Pete read. Under those words, engraved on the medal, was the name "Peter Phillips." Pete's dad.

"Wow!" Pete said, feeling the raised letters of his dad's name. "I never knew you won any medals."

"I won these in high school," his dad said. "And a few in college, too. I won't be winning any more medals. But maybe you will one day. Whether or not you do, you'll always be a winner to me."

Pete laid his head on his father's knee. "I love you, Dad," Pete whispered. "I wouldn't trade you for any other dad in the world."

THE NEXT DAY when Pete got home, he could hardly believe his eyes. The backyard looked like a racetrack. Boxes were set up like hurdles, and red cones marked the starting and finish lines.

Pete's dad leaned on his cane, a stopwatch around his neck.

"Who did all this?" Pete asked.

"Hey!" his dad grinned. "I may not have fast legs, but I can still teach you a few things about running."

Pete's dad told him how to stretch his legs before a race. "Now, the most important thing to remember is to always look ahead," his dad said.

"Right, Dad," Pete said, bending into a crouch and raising his head.

"On your mark, get set, GO!" his dad called out.

PETE TOOK OFF. He raced around the track, leaping over the boxes with no problem at all. He burst across the finish line.

"And the winner is, Pete Phillips!" Pete's dad shouted.

Pete trotted over to his dad and wrapped his arms around him. His dad slipped something around Pete's neck. It was the medal with his dad's name in raised letters. Peter Phillips. Pete's name.

"Always look ahead," Pete said. Pete's dad put both arms around his son. For just a moment, he didn't even need his cane.

When a Parent is Chronically Ill

One of a child's worst fears is the fear of losing a parent. When a parent gets very sick, this fear increases. Along with fear, a child will often feel anger. You can feel the concern and the anger when Pete says, "But why would God give you fast legs and then take them away from you?" Pete's dad is right not to blame God, but rather to focus on God's presence in his life and to recognize that God gives us strength to deal with life and with death.

Notice that Pete's dad did not sugarcoat reality. Rather he admits that he is ill. Moreover he goes on to remind Pete that God is there with both of them and God gives emotional strength in the face of physical weakness.

You can use this book to address the illness of any person close to your child—a parent, a sibling, an extended relative, a grandparent, or a friend. The truths emphasized in this story are the same. God loves us, God is there for us, God gives us strength, *no matter what.*

As you read *When Pete's Dad Got Sick* with your child, remember the following:

- Talk to your child about the illness. You don't have to go into detail, but as best as you can, let your child know what is going on now and what is likely to happen.
- Help your child to remember that he or she is safe and is not going to get

sick like this. While this fact might seem obvious to you, it is not always so obvious to a child.

- Create an atmosphere of truthful optimism. Perhaps with this illness there will be times of remission. If so, tell your child. Remind your child of the fact that keeps Christians ultimately optimistic, the fact that God gives us strength and eternal life with him.
- Let your child know that God understands when we worry. God also understands our anger, even when we get angry with him. If we parents can understand our child's anger and frustration even when it is directed toward us, how much more does God understand our anger when we are frustrated because we don't understand his plan.
- Remind your child to expect good things and fun times even when someone your child loves is sick. With humor, optimism, and reality Pete's dad reminded Pete of something much more important than his illness. He reminded Pete how precious he is to Pete's dad and to God. He also reminded Pete that he has a future, and he has good things in life he can look forward to.

The truths expressed in this book are encouraging to God's children of any age. As you read and re-read this book, keep that in mind.

A Word to Parents and Other Caregivers

Everyday life in God's world presents challenges and problems for all of us. Children, as well as adults, struggle with a variety of feelings when faced with emotionally charged situations. By helping our children clearly recognize God's loving presence in their lives—that he is with them no matter what happens—we help to prepare them for life. One of the names of Jesus Christ is "Emanuel, God with us," and God with us is the pervasive theme of this Helping Kids Heal series. The books honestly and sensitively address the difficult emotions children face.

Children love a good story, and stories can provide a safe way to approach issues, concerns, and problems. Therapists who work with children have long used stories to help children acknowledge emotions they would rather avoid. When a loving parent, a kind grandparent, or a caring teacher reads about a story character who is experiencing difficult feelings, the child has permission to feel, to ask questions, to voice his or her fears, and to struggle with emotions. Remember, as with any good story, one reading is never enough. Repetition is a great reminder of the truths contained in the story.

Each child is different. Some children, when facing a difficult emotion, will ask questions and wonder aloud about the characters in the books. Other children are content to just listen and take it all in. After several readings, try to draw them out to talk about the story. You, more than anyone else, will know what the child needs. Keep these things in mind as you use these books:

- God is with you, too. You may be reading about something that is close to your heart. Your emotions may be as tender as the child's as you read the story. Pray that you will have a sense of God's loving presence in your heart.
- You do not have to know the perfect answer for every question, nor do you have to answer all of the child's questions. Some of the best questions are the hardest to answer. Be sure, however, to acknowledge the child's question. Be honest. Say that you don't have the answer. If the child asks, "Why did she have to die?" it's all right to say, "I don't know."
- Pray with the child to feel God's loving presence. Let the child know that you care about him or her and about his or her feelings. Let the child know that whether he or she feels God's presence or not, God is still with him or her. This is a loving, precious, and powerful gift that you can give the child.
- Be aware that God works in a variety of ways. You may not get much of a response from the child as you read this book. Don't be concerned. Read the book at different times. You are planting a seed—a seed for the child to recognize God is at work in everyone's life.
- Have fun! Enjoy the story and this time with the child. Children are precious gifts from God created in his image. God is helping you to prepare the child for a future in his kingdom.

Dr. Scott

R. Scott Stehouwer, Ph.D., professor of psychology, Calvin College, and clinical psychologist